RATS... THE CITY'S CRAWLIN' WITH 'EM.
BIG ONES
LITTLE ONES
REALLY BIG ONES
SPLISH
LITTLE ONES...
RAT BANE
BUT IT DOESN'T MATTER.
BECAUSE TONIGHT, THEY'RE—
DUFF! WHY ARE YA STANDING IN THE RAIN?
WAIT... ARE YOU BROODING?
S L S A
I0572624

OH, HI THE CAPTAIN! I WAS JUST DOING SOME NARRATING.
NARRATING?
YEAH!
SNRF
MREOW!!!

THAT'S NOT... LISTEN, I NEED YOU FOCUSED, YA HEAR? THIS IS YOUR BIG JOB.
- SMUSH -
I THOUGHT THE HEALTH PEOPLE SHUT THIS PLACE DOWN BECAUSE OF ALL THE...
THE SCAMPERING RAT
...RATS.
THAT THEY DID. I CAN DEAL WITH BIG RULE-BREAKERS. YOU'VE GOTTA TAKE CARE OF THE SMALLER ONES AND...
NOTICE
CLOSED
BUZZ OFF
EHH, WHERE'S YOUR SWORD?

I DIDN'T BRING IT! THE GUYS AT THE BARRACKS GAVE ME RAT BANE INSTEAD!
THAT'S JUST A MASON'S HAMMER.
IT'S RAT BANE!
IT'S FOR MASONS.
IT'S FOR SOLDIERS.
GUARDS, NOT SOLDIERS AND THE GUYS, THEY MIGHT... UH.
IT'S FINE. THEY'RE JUST RATS...
THE CELLAR DOOR IS AROUND THE BACK, I'LL CLEAR OUT THE RABBLE UP HERE, AND YOU—
BANE SOME RATS!
HEE HEE HEE!
BANE SOME... RATS...
CRASH!!
TIME TO CLEAR OUT THE DRUNKS.
OFF!

DUFF OPENED THE DOOR TO THE BASEMENT.
CREEEAK
HIS JOB? USE HIS MIGHTY HAMMER TO SMITE THE...
THUMP THUMP THUMP
RATS...
WHERE DO I EVEN START?
ZZZZ
HMM?
??
ACK!!
THUD!!!

TASTE!
CRACK-
THE!
KSH
SMASH
HAMMER!

THIS IS HARD.
COULD YOU GUYS
JUST SCAMPER A
LITTLE SLOWER?
CREEAK
FIRE WINE
CLATTER
CLATTER
CLATTER
FWOOSH

GOTCHA, YOU LITTLE UH... RAT!
FWAP
!
SEE, THE GUYS AT THE BARRACKS... I DON'T THINK THEY REALLY THINK I'M GOOD AT THIS GUARD STUFF...
?
I ACTUALLY WISH I DIDN'T HAVE TO DO THIS, BUT...
THE CAPTAIN HAS MY BACK, BUT THE REST OF THEM—I DON'T KNOW.
BUT THIS IS WHERE I TURN IT AROUND.
SQUEAK!
SHOW 'EM ALL
SQUEAK! SQUEAK! SQUEAK!
I'M JUST AS MUCH A GUARD AS—
SQUEAK, SQUEAK!
WHAT ARE YOU DOING WITH YOUR LITTLE ARMS?
...AND STAY OUT THIS TIME YA—
KEEP

KEEP OUT!!!
BOOM

DUFF?
CAN YOU HEAR ME?
DUFF!!!

WAKE UP, DUFF!
GRAH...
ARE YOU OKAY? WHAT HAPPENED DOWN THERE? DUFF?
WHOAH! COOL. HEY THE CAPTAIN, YOU SEEIN' THIS?
YEAH, I'M SEEING THIS.
THE EXPLOSION LOOKS LIKE IT CAME FROM THE BASEMENT.

WAIT... THE BASEMENT?
THAT MEANS...

THAT THE EXPLOSION...

KILLED ALL THE RATS!

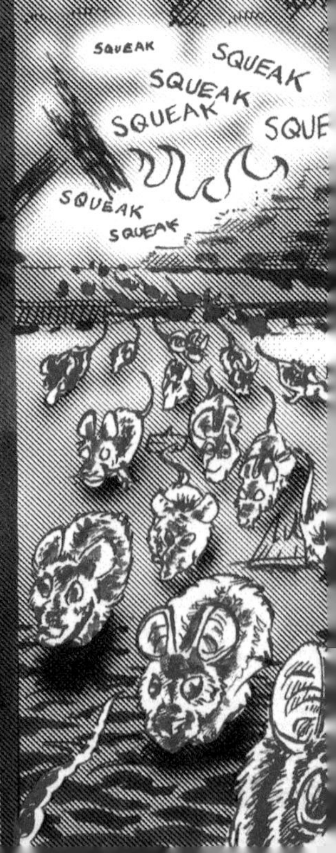

SQUEAK
SQUEAK
SQUEAK
SQUEAK
SQUE
SQUEAK
SQUEAK

UGH.
LISTEN, DUFF,
MY BOY, I—
MAKE WAY!
TOOK THEM LONG ENOUGH.
DUFF. I'LL HANDLE THIS.
MAKE WAY!
WELL MET...
GORGE...
CHAB...
AND RENN,
OF COURSE...

NOT TO WORRY, CITIZENS! BACK TO YOUR HOMES.
LIGHT BE DAMNED, WHAT IS GOING ON?
THERE APPEAR TO BE NO CASUALTIES. THE BUILDING WAS CLEAR, THANKFULLY.
SOMETHING CAUSED AN EXPLOSION. HAVEN'T HAD A MOMENT TO CHECK, BUT—
SOME THING -OR- SOME ONE?
HMM...

YOU CAN`T PROTECT HIM FOREVER, CAPTAIN. ONCE WORD OF THIS GETS BACK TO DOVAEL—
THE REAL CAPTAIN—
—HE`S GONE! FOR GOOD, THIS TIME.
WELL MAYBE IF YOU FOOLS HADN`T GIVEN HIM "RAT BANE" HE WOULDN`T HAVE HAD ANY ISSUES!
OH PLEASE, THEY`RE RATS. A HAMMER SHOULD HAVE BEEN FINE. IT WAS "RAT BANE," AFTER ALL.
CRUNCH
UH... GUYS...
PLUS, DO YOU REALLY TRUST DOOF—ER, DUFF—WITH SOMETHING POINTY?
I`M SURE THAT WILL GO OVER REAL WELL WITH DOVAEL. THIS IS ON YOUR HEAD IF IT`S ON HIS, WHICH WE DON`T EVEN KNOW FOR SURE...

I DON'T THINK THERE WERE ANY STAIRS HERE BEFORE...
HEY GUYS!
I MAY NOT BE "CAPTAIN" ANY LONGER, BUT I'VE BEEN DOING THIS A LOT LONGER THAN YOU. I WORKED WITH—
"I WORKED WITH YOUR FATHER, AND IF HE SAW THE BLAH BLAH."
I'VE HEARD THIS SONG BEFORE CAPTAIN. MIGHT WORK ON SOME OF THE OTHERS, BUT NOT ME. THAT PET OF YOURS IS—
SEE?
EXPLOSION MUST HAVE OPENED IT UP...
GUYS! I FOUND A HOLE!
OR MAYBE ITS THE BASEMENT, EVER THINK OF THAT?
WHO CARES? IT'S JUST A HOLE.
DARK DOWN THERE.
GRAB SOME TORCHES.

LIGHT BE DAMNED I'M LETTING YOU DOWN HERE ALONE. DON'T WANT ANOTHER WAYWARD INN.
THEY NEVER PROVED THAT WAS ME.
HOW BIG IS THIS PLACE?
WHERE ARE WE?
CRASH!

BENDARIN IN THE STONE.
I NEVER THOUGHT I'D SEE IT WITH MY OWN EYES...
WE NEED TO GO BACK.
CREAK
CRUMBLE
NOT UNTIL WE SEE WHAT'S IN THERE!
CREAK
RUMBLE
I'M NOT SURE THIS IS SAFE!
SEE? SHAKING STOPPED. I KNEW IT WOULD. AND... WAIT...
CRICK

NOW WAIT, BEFORE YA GET ALL GRABBY...
WE ARE OVERMINE'S PRIDE.
WE GUARD THE CITY ABOVE THE MOUNTAIN.
WE DO NOT — NONE OF YOU ARE LISTENING, ARE YOU?
I'M LISTENING, THE CAPTAIN.
THANK YOU, DUFF.
RUMBLE
THAT SWORD...
I CAN SENSE IT. IT'S MAGICAL...
WE DON'T KNOW WHAT THIS IS. WHOSE IT IS
BE SMART, GORGE.

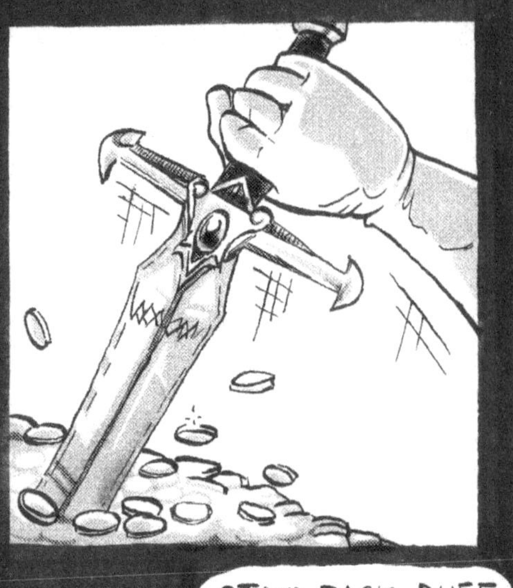

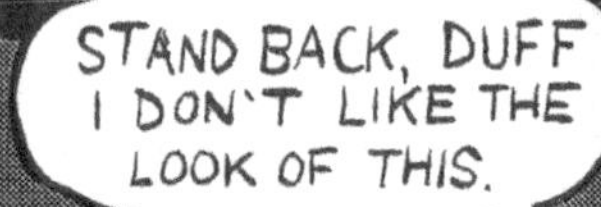
STAND BACK, DUFF
I DON'T LIKE THE
LOOK OF THIS.

NEARLY ALL OF THE
ENCHANTED WEAPONS WERE
DESTROYED OR LOST AFTER
THE WAR — AND THE UPRISING...

WITH THIS, I CAN
EXACT MY REVENGE...

TAKING CONTROL OF OVERMINE WILL BE EASY.
I WON'T BE NEEDING YOU ANYMORE.
I NEVER ACTUALLY NEEDED YOU IN THE FIRST PLACE.
I'LL SEE THAT YOU'RE "RETIRED."
AND YOU, HEH... I'VE BEEN WAITING FOR A CHANCE TO—

SPLORCH

THOOSH

DO YOU THINK IF SHE WAS WEARING HER HELMET SHE—
LET'S GO!!!
RUMBLE
RUMBLE

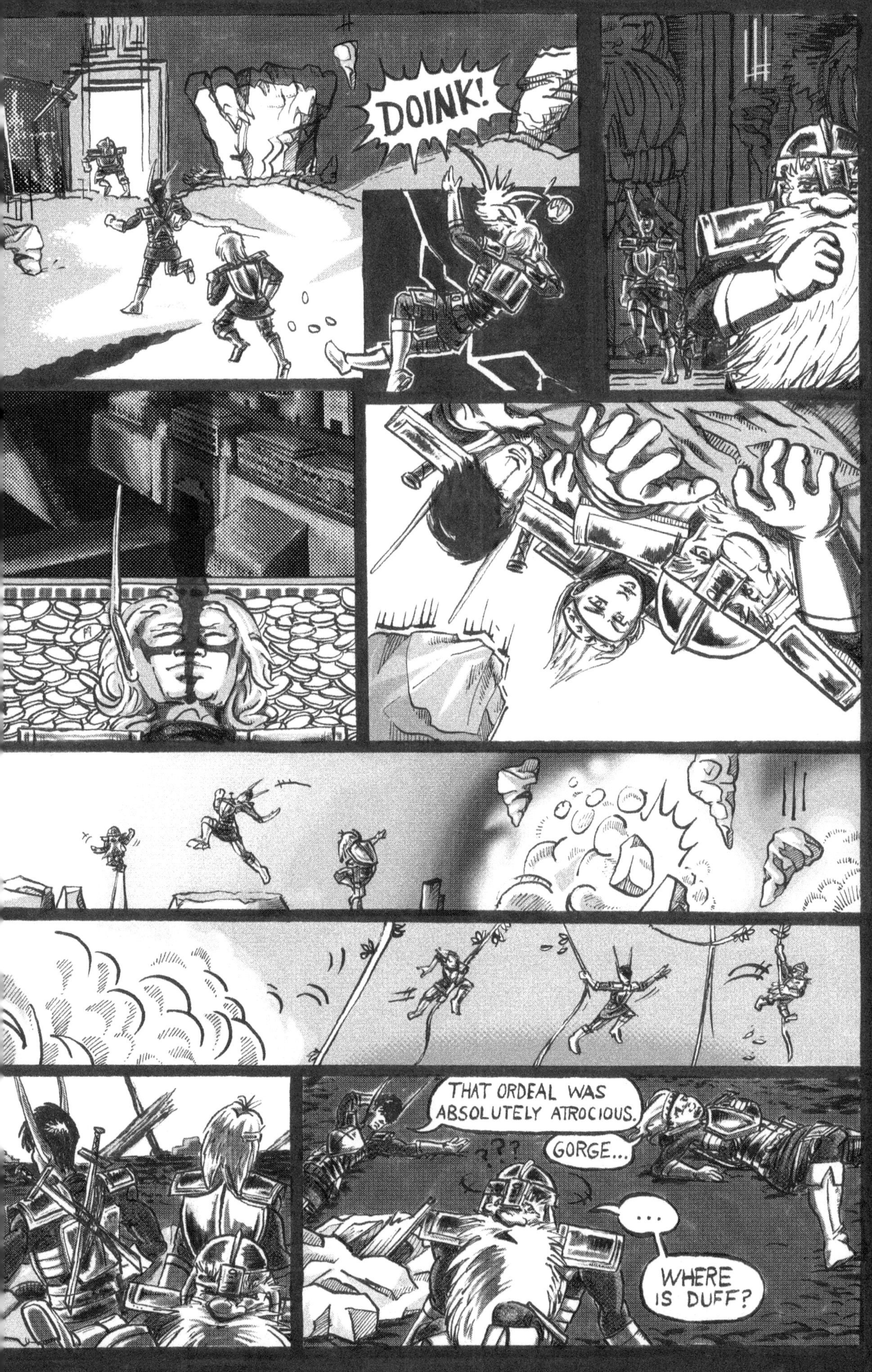

DOINK!
THAT ORDEAL WAS ABSOLUTELY ATROCIOUS.
GORGE...
???
...
WHERE IS DUFF?

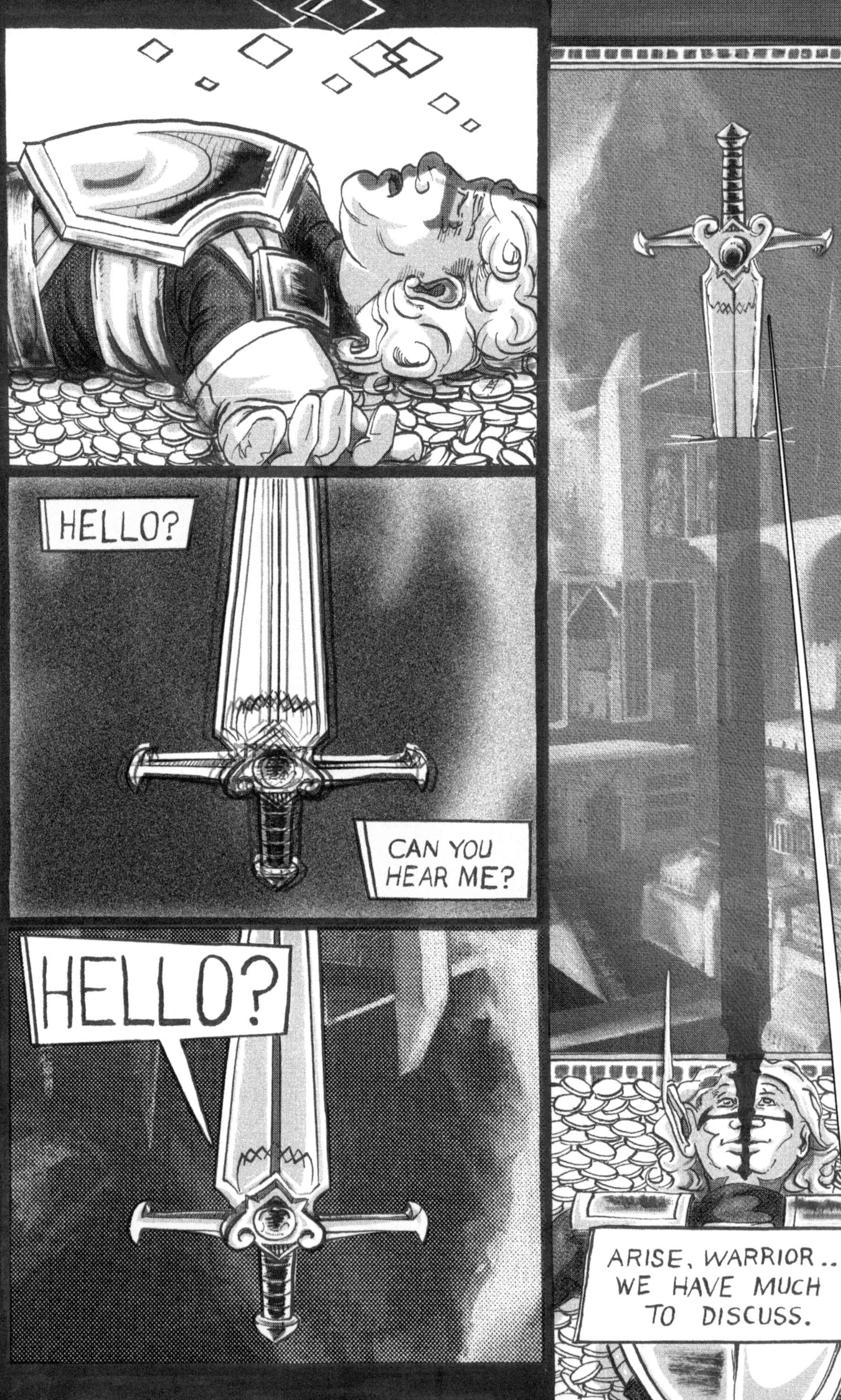
HELLO?
CAN YOU HEAR ME?
HELLO?
ARISE, WARRIOR...
WE HAVE MUCH TO DISCUSS.